Same-Different

Fairy Tales Edition

A Cooperative Game for Analytic Thinking Skills

Spencer Kagan, Ph.D.

Illustrated by Celso Rodriguez

Kagan

Kagan Publishing
981 Calle Amanecer
San Clemente, CA 92673
1 (800) 933-2667
Fax: (949) 545-6301
www.KaganOnline.com

ISBN: 978-1-879097-44-5

Same-Different

Table of Contents

Same-Different

The concept of **Same-Different** is simple, yet powerful. Students sit across from each other with a file folder barrier between them. Each student looks at only one of the two pictures. Without seeing what his or her partner sees, they must discover the what's the same and what's different between the two pictures. Students of any age quickly become totally engrossed as they play **Same-Different**. It is an immediate favorite.

Same-Different Develops Multiple Intelligences

In spite of the deceptive simplicity of the structure and the immediate fun, game-like atmosphere among students while engaged in **Same-Different** activities, as students play **Same-Different** they simultaneously develop a number of intelligences.

Verbal/Linguistic Intelligence

Same-Different is a terrific way to develop the verbal/linguistic intelligence. Students must communicate clearly and effectively to find all the similarities and differences. **Same-Different** works especially well for ESL students and students learning a second language. Students build vocabu-

lary as they describe their pictures, communicate in context, and communicate in comprehensible terms. Students also practice writing skills as they record their answers.

Logical/Mathematical Intelligence

Students develop analytic thinking skills as they look carefully at the details of the illustrations, breaking them into component parts trying to uncover the differences.

Visual/Spatial Intelligence

Students work on spatial awareness and directionality as they examine the illustrations in detail.

Interpersonal Intelligence

Students must cooperate to find the similarities and differences. Students learn to "take role of the other"—they learn to distinguish their own from another person's point of view. Bonding between students emerges. The bonding between students is fostered because of the strong positive interdependence created by the structure. Neither student can succeed without the active cooperation of the other, so success is viewed as a success of the pair. Further, because the pictures contain "easy to discover" as well as "difficult to discover" differences, the task ensures success for everyone, while remaining challenging for all.

Naturalist Intelligence

The core operation of the naturalist intelligence is discrimination of natural and non-natural objects and phenomena. Students develop discriminatory skills as they closely examine the illustrations.

A Little History

To my knowledge Judy Winn-Bell Olsen's book, *Look Again Pictures* (Alemany Press, 1984) was the first publication of a set of pictures which differ in key respects. The book was designed to promote language development and acquisition among students limited in English proficiency.

Early on in developing my approach to training teachers in Cooperative Learning, I began to emphasize the importance of structures. I learned that if I gave teachers five good cooperative learning activities, I was likely to get a phone call after a week, the message being, "I tried those activities last week and they were great! What do I do next week?" In contrast, if I gave the teachers five good structures, they would have an unlimited number of activities for their classrooms because any one structure can be used with a range of curriculum to generate an infinite number of activities.

Thus, when I told teachers about *Look Again Pictures* and had them try a pair of pictures, I would always have them brainstorm other content they could adapt to the structure.

There was no shortage of ideas — teachers immediately saw how the structure could be adapted to improve skills in geography, science, language arts, math, social studies and other subject areas. With great enthusiasm in workshops they produced lists of possible applications for the **Same-Different** structure.

Initially I was quite excited by this outpouring of ideas. But when I checked later to see which of the ideas had actually been implemented, only the exceptional teacher went the next step and made new activities to use in **Same-Different**.

This experience was different from the experience I had with structures which were not materials-based. For example, when teachers learned Three-Step Interview in a workshop, many readily used the structure in science, math, social studies, literature, and other subjects.

Eventually I concluded that it was unfair to expect teachers to spend their days teaching and their nights producing new curriculum materials. I realized that if **Same-Different** (and other materials-based structures) were to be broadly implemented, support materials needed to be made readily available. Thus the birth of ready-to-use **Same-Different** activity books.

In This Book

In this book, you will find all the materials necessary to play **Same-Different** with fairy tales. Included are two reproducible illustrations for each of fifteen fairy tales, recording sheets and keys. The pictures pairs have at least 20 differences. Students record the similarities and the differences on the recording sheet and check their answers with the key.

Acknowledgments

Celso Rodriguez did the original artwork for this book **Karen Schumacher** hand-colored and with **Miguel Kagan** designed the cover and spent many dedicated hours at the computer transforming the artwork into **Same-Different** pictures. Their efforts translate into hours of enjoyable and enriching educational experiences for students of all ages.

Spencer Kagan

Spencer Kagan, Ph.D.
July, 1997

Preparing for
Same-Different

Materials You'll Need

★ Picture 1 and Picture 2

Students work in pairs to find 20 differences and 20 similarities between Picture 1 and Picture 2. This book includes picture pairs for fifteen fairy tales. Photocopy Picture 1 for half of the class and Picture 2 for the other half.

Hints: If possible, copy Picture 1 on one color card-stock and Picture 2 on another color. Using different colors makes it easy to keep the two different illustrations separate for passing them out to students and collecting them. If you intend to use the activity over and over with your class or do it for many years, laminate the card stock illustrations.

★ Recording Sheet

Students use the recording sheet to record similarities and differences. Photocopy one recording sheet for each pair on plain white paper. There is one recording sheet with each fairy tale and extras in the back of the book.

★ Key

After students have found all the similarities and differences or can find no more, they check their answers against the key. The key for each fairy tale is located after the picture pairs. If you are working with the whole class at the same time, you can photocopy the key on a transparency and project it for the class. If students are working independently, at centers, or at different rates, copy a key for each pair.

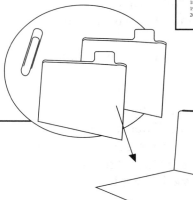

★ File Folder Barrier

Students work on opposite sides of a barrier. File folder barriers are easy to make. Paper clip the top of two file folders together and spread the base for a self-standing barrier.

Same-Different: Fairy Tales© • Kagan Publishing • 1 (800) 933-2667

4

Helpful Hints...

Model Same-Different

If you take a minute to model how to play **Same-Different**, it will go much smoother and result in more equal participation, especially for younger students. With the class watching, set up a file folder barrier. Role play with a student:

Teacher: "My picture of *The Lion and the Mouse* has trees in the background."

Student: "Mine too."

Teacher: "Since that is a similarity, I will record it on the recording sheet under the 'Same' column." Record the similarity.

Then, get more specific: "Do you have two trees on the left side of the lion?"

Student: "No I have four trees."

Teacher: "Since that is a difference, I will write 'Number of trees' in the 'Different' column."

After recording, pass the recording sheet to your partner. "Now you ask me a question." Let him or her record the next answer.

Use Reflection Time

After students play for a while, have them reflect on their interaction.

"Put down your pencils, please. Do not show each other your pictures. I want you to stop talking about the pictures and discuss your process — how you are going about solving this task. In some pairs only one person is asking all the questions and the other person is answering. In other pairs both people are asking and answering questions. How are you tackling the task? In some pairs students are taking time to provide each other a general description of their picture before trying to find differences. Other pairs jumped right in trying to find differences. Please reflect on your strategy and experiment with it. For example, if one person is asking the questions and the other is answering, switch roles. If only one person is recording all the differences, take turns, or let the other person record for awhile."

Same-Different

A pair is given two similar illustrations of the same fairy tale, and a recording sheet. Students work together to discover everything that is the same and everything that is different in the two illustrations. The challenge: Neither student can see the other's illustration.

Students form pairs. They build a barrier between them, then each get a different illustration of the same fairy tale. There are twenty differences. The illustrations have some elements that are missing, modified, colored, moved, or added. The partner's work on opposite sides of their file folder barrier to discover the similarities and differences between the two fairy tale pictures. Students take turns recording each similarity or difference on their recording sheet. After they think they have uncovered all the similarities and differences or can't find any more, they set the two illustrations side by side and check to make sure everything they listed is accurate. They can continue to find more similarities and differences as they both look at both illustrations. When all done, students compare their recording sheet with the key.

1 Pairs Build Buddy Barriers

Pairs will need a barrier so each cannot see each other's illustration. File folder barriers are very simple to build. Give each team two file folders and one paper clip. They clip the file folders together at the top with a paper clip and spread the base to make a stand-alone buddy barrier.

2 Distribute Materials

Make enough copies of Picture 1 and 2. Once students have their barriers in place, have Student A's come up to receive Picture 1. Make sure they do not show Student B their picture. Then have Student B's come up and bring back Picture 2 and a recording sheet.

4 Students Compare Pictures

When the pair has uncovered all the similarities and differences, or can't find any more, they take down the barrier and set the two pictures side by side to compare the pictures. They go over all the similarities and differences they recorded and make sure they are accurate. Then, they continue to find more similarities and differences. Student check their answers with the key.

3 Students Discover Similarities & Differences

The pair works together to discover everything that is the same and everything that is different about the two items. Students take turns recording the similarities and differences.

Easy Buddy Barriers...

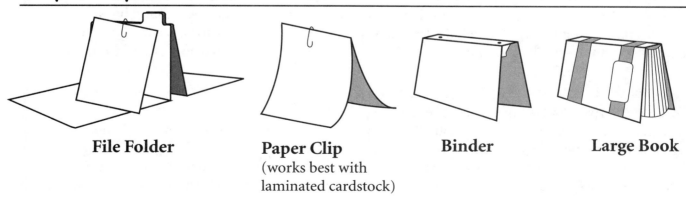

File Folder

Paper Clip
(works best with laminated cardstock)

Binder

Large Book

...or have students sit back to back

Variations for
Same-Different

There are a number of ways to play Same-Different. Try some of these variations.

Team Same-Different

Team Same-Different

Instead of playing in pairs, have students play as a team of four with two students on each side of the barrier. After some unstructured interaction time, the teams are asked to reflect on their process and then try an experiment to change it. For example, in most teams, one student does most of the talking. Students are asked to discover who that is, and to switch roles.

Class Same-Different

For younger students, try **Same-Different** with the entire class. Half the class has access to one item and the other half to another item. The whole class works together to find the similarities and differences.

Learning Centers

Have **Same-Different** set up at a learning center. Students can play in pairs or in teams of four. Students can have a few different pictures to chose from, or they can rotate to a different learning center to do a different picture each day.

Switching Pictures

After students have worked for about five minutes, have them switch pictures to complete the task.

For the Little Ones

Students who cannot write can record differences by marking right on copies of the **Same-Different** picture. Laminated copies can be reused if students write with a dry marker or a water-based overhead marker.

Cooperative Format

The number of differences found by pairs or teams are summed, adding toward a class goal. Each team or pair is appreciated for its contribution to the class goal.

Competitive Format

Pairs or teams are given a limited amount of time and are encouraged to find as many differences as they can. Those who find the most are recognized. Those with successful strategies are encouraged to explain their strategies to others.

Developing Communication Strategies

Half the pairs in the class are instructed to use one communication strategy, for example to ask only "Yes-No" questions. The other half are encouraged to use another strategy, say, to spend a full minute each way describing the picture as completely as they can before asking any questions. The outcomes of the two strategies are contrasted as well as the feelings of the team members using each method. Principles about communication are inferred.

Memory Only

Students are each given from two to five minutes to look at their pictures. The pictures are set aside. They then see how many differences they can discover as a pair working from memory only.

Passing Notes

Students are not allowed to speak. They pass notes back and forth to discover what's the same and what's different. They can ask questions in their notes or provide descriptions, but they cannot speak.

Physical Objects

Students may play same-different with similar physical objects on each side of the barrier such as a butterfly and a moth, two leaves, two plants, or even two specimens to view with a magnifying glass or microscope.

The Writing Challenge

Students are given about ten minutes to write as full a description of their picture as they can. They then trade their descriptive writing with a partner who was writing about the other picture. Students are not allowed to speak. They each find as many differences as they can by comparing their own picture with the written description of the other picture provided by their partner. Students are encouraged to reflect on their attempts, and to develop and record writing strategies which might help them be more successful in future attempts. They can produce edited versions to try on another receiver to view the effects of their editing.

Non-Visual Formats

Same-Different can be played with other modes of information, such as auditory (students listen to different versions of a song or poem); and kinesthetic (students put their hands into different boxes to feel cubes, cones, and spheres).

The Writing Challenge

Making Your Own
Same-Different
Activities

It is easy to make your own **Same-Different** activities for whatever you are studying. Here are a few ideas you may want to try. On the opposite page are ideas for using **Same-Different** across the curriculum.

1. White-Out

Take a drawing, clip art, map, photo, or written material. Make two copies. Use white-out to subtract items and a black marker to add items to Copy 1. Add and subtract different items to Copy 2. Use the two altered copies as originals and make copies for your class. Make some things you add and subtract to each picture very obvious and others very subtle so there will be success for all and a challenge for all. As you make copies, use a different color paper for each original to make management easier.

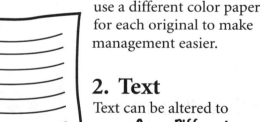

2. Text

Text can be altered to create **Same-Different** materials. For example, one teacher made two copies of a page from her science text which described crocodiles and alligators. From one copy she removed all description of crocodiles. She took out all description of alligators from the other. The **Same-Different** answer sheet asked compare-contrast questions about crocodiles and alligators so students had to read the copies carefully to each other to be successful. You can also use stories or similar articles.

3. Photographs

Use two similar magazine pictures. Have students find how they are the same and how they are different. You can also make your own photographs. Arrange objects in a scene. Take a picture.  Rearrange the objects in the scene. Take a second picture. Use the enlarging photocopier on resulting copies to create two master copies and then make copies of each for classroom use.

Photo Hint: Place your camera on a tripod and keep the outside margins of the photo the same to make only the objects and not the perspective change.

4. Miscellaneous Materials

All sorts of materials work well for **Same-Different**. You can use two songs, advertisements, foods, soft drink cans, rocks, plants, textures, books, problems, films. The basic idea remains the same. Each student only has access to one item. By talking they try to discover all the ways the objects are the same or different.

General Hint

To ensure success and a challenge for all, include in each Same-Different activity some differences which will be obvious for the slowest achievers and some which will be difficult for the highest achievers. The remaining differences should be distributed between the extremes.

Same-Different: Fairy Tales© • Kagan Publishing • 1 (800) 933-2667

Ideas Across the Curriculum

Math

- Geometric shapes arranged differently
- Counting number of objects (primary)
- Pictures of three dimensional objects viewed from different angles
- Outcomes depicted within two different pie graphs
- Outcomes depicted in a pie vs. a bar graph
- Sizes (centimeter vs. inch conversions)
- Patterns
- Pictures of tangrams arranged differently

Language Arts

- Crossword puzzles (One with Down filled in; the other with Across filled in)
- Passages written in different verb tenses
- Passages with different verbs (or adverbs, or adjectives)
- Passages punctuated differently
- Subjective vs. Objective Writing Samples
- Show vs. tell writing samples
- Edited vs. unedited passages
- Passages edited in different styles
- Photos with items rearranged (for vocabulary development). Two photos of a dinner setting — for development of food vocabulary
- Business vs. personal letter style
- Forms of sentence structure or sentence combining
- Proofreading for punctuation
- Two fairy tale versions
- Two characters from novel (one student reads about Tom Sawyer; the other reads about Huck Finn.)
- Students first write a story in their own words (e.g. The Tortoise and the Hare) and then pass their versions to other students to play Same-Different.

Art

- Two Impressionistic paintings
- Paintings in different styles
- Photos developed differently
- Music written at different rate or key
- Coloring book pictures colored differently

Science

- Comparative anatomy (e.g. skeletal systems)
- Verbal descriptions of similar animals (dinosaurs, dogs, lizards) or plants (leaf structures)
- Plant vs. animal cells
- Seasonal changes
- Maps with different features
- Butterfly vs. Moth; Crocodile vs. Alligator
- Pictures of Ecosystems
- Atomic structures

Social Science

- Community workers (policemen or firemen)
- Architectural styles
- Dwellings of Indians
- Cultural differences in dress, body language
- Urban - Rural scenes
- Pictures, photos from different time periods
- Maps before and after certain wars
- Passages about two events (World War I and II)
- Civil War soldiers North vs. South (pictures)
- Plantation owner vs. slave
- Views: Abe Lincoln vs. George Washington

Part 2

Fairy Tales

Cinderella

Cinderella

Cinderella

Answer Sheet

Same

Different

	Same		Different
1.	_____	1.	_____
2.	_____	2.	_____
3.	_____	3.	_____
4.	_____	4.	_____
5.	_____	5.	_____
6.	_____	6.	_____
7.	_____	7.	_____
8.	_____	8.	_____
9.	_____	9.	_____
10.	_____	10.	_____
11.	_____	11.	_____
12.	_____	12.	_____
13.	_____	13.	_____
14.	_____	14.	_____
15.	_____	15.	_____
16.	_____	16.	_____
17.	_____	17.	_____
18.	_____	18.	_____
19.	_____	19.	_____
20.	_____	20.	_____

Same-Different: Fairy Tales® • Kagan Publishing • 1 (800) 933-2667

Cinderella
Key

1. Stars insky

2. Position of moon

3. Color of Cinderella's dress

4. Cinderella's purse

5. Candle flame

6. Color of pumpkin coach stem

7. Color pumpkin coach seat

8. Position of worm in hole

9. Color of Fairy God Mother's sleeves

10. Color of stars on Fairy God Mother's dress

11. Number of stars on Fairy God Mother's dress

12. Bow on Fairy God Mother's dress

13. Bow strings on Fairy God Mother's dress

14. Fairy God Mother's wand

15. Fairy God Mother's feet

16. Flowers on ground

17. Cinderella's necklace

18. Number of bells on pumpkin coach

19. Handle on door

20. Pocket on Fairy God Mother's dress

The City Mouse
and the Country Mouse

The City Mouse
and the Country Mouse

The City Mouse and the Country Mouse

Answer Sheet

Same

1. _____
2. _____
3. _____
4. _____
5. _____
6. _____
7. _____
8. _____
9. _____
10. _____
11. _____
12. _____
13. _____
14. _____
15. _____
16. _____
17. _____
18. _____
19. _____
20. _____

Different

1. _____
2. _____
3. _____
4. _____
5. _____
6. _____
7. _____
8. _____
9. _____
10. _____
11. _____
12. _____
13. _____
14. _____
15. _____
16. _____
17. _____
18. _____
19. _____
20. _____

The City Mouse and the Country Mouse
Key

1. Color of street light

2. Walk/don't walk signal

3. Walk signal button

4. Number of stars in sky

5. Color of City Mouse's tuxedo

6. Position of moon

7. Color of City Mouse's hat

8. Position of sun

9. Color of City Mouse's shoes

10. Position of cellular phone

11. City Mouse's coat pocket/flower

12. Position of patch on Country Mouse's pants

13. Amount of grass on ground

14. Position of worm in ground

15. Color of arrows

16. Number of trees on hill

17. Hood ornament on car

18. Number of windows on building

19. Country Mouse's tie

20. Number of egg baskets

The Frog Prince

The Frog Prince

The Frog Prince

Answer Sheet

Same

1. _____
2. _____
3. _____
4. _____
5. _____
6. _____
7. _____
8. _____
9. _____
10. _____
11. _____
12. _____
13. _____
14. _____
15. _____
16. _____
17. _____
18. _____
19. _____
20. _____

Different

1. _____
2. _____
3. _____
4. _____
5. _____
6. _____
7. _____
8. _____
9. _____
10. _____
11. _____
12. _____
13. _____
14. _____
15. _____
16. _____
17. _____
18. _____
19. _____
20. _____

The Frog Prince
Key

1. Number of warts on frog

2. Curls in Princess' hair

3. Position of sun

4. Number of clouds in sky

5. Flowers on left hill

6. Flower between rocks on left

7. Number of rocks on left

8. Water Pitcher on left side of well

9. Color of Prince's boots

10. Number of buttons on Prince's boots

11. Color of knife

12. Shape of knife handles

13. Freckles on Prince's face

14. Color of Prince's vest

15. Hill between Prince and Princess

16. Color of Princess' dress

17. Ruffles and pleats on Princess' sleeves

18. Stripe at bottom of Princess' dress

19. Mouse hole on left side of water well

20. Position of Prince's left arm

Goldilocks and the
Three Bears

Picture 2

Goldilocks and the Three Bears

Goldilocks and
the Three Bears
Answer Sheet

Same		Different	
1.	_____	1.	_____
2.	_____	2.	_____
3.	_____	3.	_____
4.	_____	4.	_____
5.	_____	5.	_____
6.	_____	6.	_____
7.	_____	7.	_____
8.	_____	8.	_____
9.	_____	9.	_____
10.	_____	10.	_____
11.	_____	11.	_____
12.	_____	12.	_____
13.	_____	13.	_____
14.	_____	14.	_____
15.	_____	15.	_____
16.	_____	16.	_____
17.	_____	17.	_____
18.	_____	18.	_____
19.	_____	19.	_____
20.	_____	20.	_____

Goldilocks and the Three Bears

Key

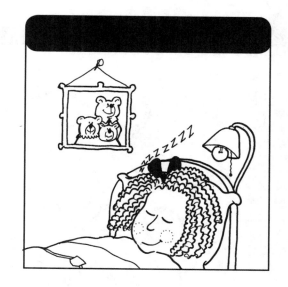

1. Position of picture frame

2. Position of light on bed

3. Goldilocks' hair bow

4. String hanging out of light

5. Number of pencils in Papa Bear's pocket

6. Papa Bear's pocket watch

7. Color of Papa Bear's pants

8. Mama Bear's apron

9. Position of shoes on floor

10. Number of socks on floor

11. Position of bowl and spoon on floor

12. Number of flowers on rug

13. Position of bat and baseball on bed frame

14. Baseballs on blanket

15. Plug in outlet

16. Number on Baby Bear's baseball shirt

17. Baseball cap on Baby Bear

18. Mama Bear's earrings

19. Buttons on Papa Bear's collar

20. Color of inside of bowl on floor

Hansel & Gretel

Hansel & Gretel

Hansel & Gretel

Answer Sheet

Same

1. _____
2. _____
3. _____
4. _____
5. _____
6. _____
7. _____
8. _____
9. _____
10. _____
11. _____
12. _____
13. _____
14. _____
15. _____
16. _____
17. _____
18. _____
19. _____
20. _____

Different

1. _____
2. _____
3. _____
4. _____
5. _____
6. _____
7. _____
8. _____
9. _____
10. _____
11. _____
12. _____
13. _____
14. _____
15. _____
16. _____
17. _____
18. _____
19. _____
20. _____

Same-Different: Fairy Tales • Kagan Publishing • 1 (800) 933-2667

Hansel & Gretel
Key

1. Number of cherries on roof

2. Position of window on roof

3. Color of window on roof

4. Position of chimney pipe

5. Position of sun

6. Color of lollipop on left

7. Small lollipop on left

8. Color of lollipop on right

9. Extra lollipop on right

10. Leaves on candy

11. Shovel on ground

12. Can on ground

13. Stripes on fourth candy flower from left

14. Number of jelly beans above window shutter

15. Color of wall above door

16. Handles on window shutters above door

17. Number of hearts on window shutters above door

18. Stripes on window shutters above door

19. Heart on door

20. Door frame

Jack and the Beanstalk

Jack and the Beanstalk

Jack and
the Beanstalk
Answer Sheet

Same

1. _____
2. _____
3. _____
4. _____
5. _____
6. _____
7. _____
8. _____
9. _____
10. _____
11. _____
12. _____
13. _____
14. _____
15. _____
16. _____
17. _____
18. _____
19. _____
20. _____

Different

1. _____
2. _____
3. _____
4. _____
5. _____
6. _____
7. _____
8. _____
9. _____
10. _____
11. _____
12. _____
13. _____
14. _____
15. _____
16. _____
17. _____
18. _____
19. _____
20. _____

Same-Different: Fairy Tales© • Kagan Publishing • 1 (800) 933-2667

Jack and the Beanstalk
Key

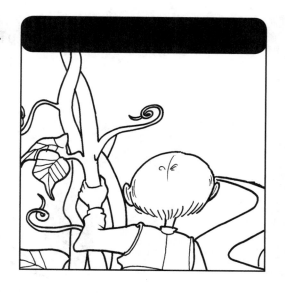

1. Number of trees

2. Position of sun

3. Dotted circles on sun

4. Roof color on castle

5. Direction of flags on castle

6. Birds in sky on left

7. Position of stars in sky

8. Number of windows on castle

9. Ladder next to cliff

10. Cave on side of cliff

11. Leaves on beanstalk

12. Stripes on Jack's pants

13. Knife in Jack's belt

14. Hole on bottom of Jack's shoe

15. Color of Jack's hair

16. Patch on Jack's pants

17. Color of Jack's sleeves

18. Color of beanstalk

19. Flower on path

20. Position of door on castle

The Lion and the Mouse

The Lion and the Mouse

The Lion and the Mouse
Answer Sheet

Same

Different

Same	Different
1. _____	1. _____
2. _____	2. _____
3. _____	3. _____
4. _____	4. _____
5. _____	5. _____
6. _____	6. _____
7. _____	7. _____
8. _____	8. _____
9. _____	9. _____
10. _____	10. _____
11. _____	11. _____
12. _____	12. _____
13. _____	13. _____
14. _____	14. _____
15. _____	15. _____
16. _____	16. _____
17. _____	17. _____
18. _____	18. _____
19. _____	19. _____
20. _____	20. _____

The Lion and the Mouse
Key

1. Number of jewels on Lion's crown

2. Position of sun

3. Position of Lion's tail

4. Number of palm trees

5. Binder between lunch pail & thermos

6. Satellite dish/antenna on top of back dirt hill

7. Satellite dish/antenna on top of front dirt hill

8. Dark shadow between ladder steps

9. Open lid on mail box

10. Flag on mail box

11. Color of Mouse's pants

12. Color of Mouse's shoes

13. Number of rocks on ground

14. Ring on Lion's paw

15. Number of points on Lion's crown

16. Color of Lion's crown

17. Floor mat outside of back dirt hill

18. Lion's toenails

19. Length of Mouse's tail

20. Lion's fangs

Little Red Riding Hood

Little Red Riding Hood

Little Red
Riding Hood

Answer Sheet

Same

Different

Same	Different
1. _____	1. _____
2. _____	2. _____
3. _____	3. _____
4. _____	4. _____
5. _____	5. _____
6. _____	6. _____
7. _____	7. _____
8. _____	8. _____
9. _____	9. _____
10. _____	10. _____
11. _____	11. _____
12. _____	12. _____
13. _____	13. _____
14. _____	14. _____
15. _____	15. _____
16. _____	16. _____
17. _____	17. _____
18. _____	18. _____
19. _____	19. _____
20. _____	20. _____

Little Red Riding Hood
Key

1. Position of slippers

2. Position of hole in floor

3. Color of blanket ruffles

4. Little Red Riding Hood's feet

5. Patch on pillow

6. Color of stripes on pillow

7. Shape on headboard

8. Position of hats on wall

9. Crack in mirror

10. Number of stars in window

11. Ends of curtain rod

12. Polka dots on curtains

13. Little Red Riding Hood's cheek

14. Outlet on wall behind bed

15. Winder on clock

16. Time on clock

17. Wolf's fangs

18. Little Red Riding Hood's apron

19. Food in basket

20. Wolf's claws

Pinocchio

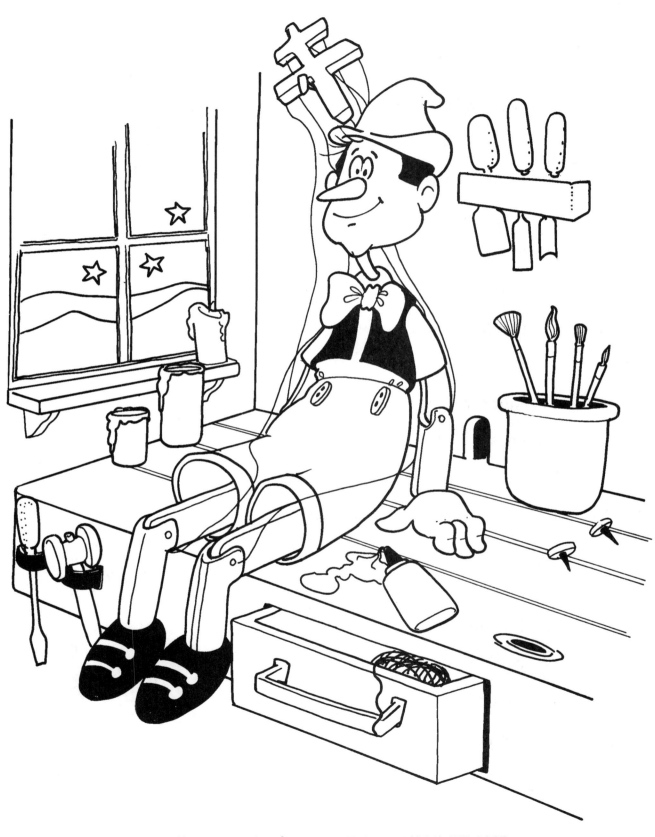

Pinocchio

Pinocchio

Answer Sheet

Same

1. _____
2. _____
3. _____
4. _____
5. _____
6. _____
7. _____
8. _____
9. _____
10. _____
11. _____
12. _____
13. _____
14. _____
15. _____
16. _____
17. _____
18. _____
19. _____
20. _____

Different

1. _____
2. _____
3. _____
4. _____
5. _____
6. _____
7. _____
8. _____
9. _____
10. _____
11. _____
12. _____
13. _____
14. _____
15. _____
16. _____
17. _____
18. _____
19. _____
20. _____

Pinocchio
Key

1. Number of stars in window

2. Number of hills in window

3. Number of candles on table

4. Flame on candle in window

5. Position of knot in table

6. Number of mouse holes in wall

7. Leaf on Pinocchio's nose

8. Polka dots on Pinocchio's bow tie

9. Color of Pinocchio's shorts

10. Number of hammers

11. Number of nails on table

12. Position of glue bottle and glue

13. Stripes on glue bottle

14. Laces on Pinocchio's shoes

15. Number of chisels hanging on wall

16. Feather in Pinocchio's hat

17. Number of brushes in jar

18. Buttons on Pinocchio's pants

19. Wood supports under window sill

20. Dowels in Pinocchio's elbow and knee joints

Rapunzel

Rapunzel

Rapunzel

Answer Sheet

Same

1. _____
2. _____
3. _____
4. _____
5. _____
6. _____
7. _____
8. _____
9. _____
10. _____
11. _____
12. _____
13. _____
14. _____
15. _____
16. _____
17. _____
18. _____
19. _____
20. _____

Different

1. _____
2. _____
3. _____
4. _____
5. _____
6. _____
7. _____
8. _____
9. _____
10. _____
11. _____
12. _____
13. _____
14. _____
15. _____
16. _____
17. _____
18. _____
19. _____
20. _____

Rapunzel
Key

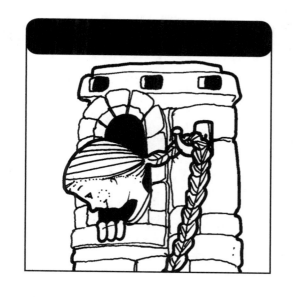

1. Bow on Rapunzel's hair

2. Holes at top of castle

3. Position of flag

4. Pattern of flag

5. Number of clouds in sky

6. Position of feather in Prince's hat

7. Shapes on Prince's sleeves

8. Color of Prince's belt

9. Position of sun

10. Number of trees on hill

11. Patch on Prince's tights

12. Color of Prince's boots

13. Number of flowers on ground

14. Position of ladder

15. Broken ladder step

16. Prince's sword

17. Rapunzel's cheek

18. Color or star on Prince's cape

19. Stairs on right bottom of castle

20. Prince's footsteps

Rumplestiltskin

Rumplestiltskin

Rumplestiltskin

Answer Sheet

Same		Different	
1.	_____	1.	_____
2.	_____	2.	_____
3.	_____	3.	_____
4.	_____	4.	_____
5.	_____	5.	_____
6.	_____	6.	_____
7.	_____	7.	_____
8.	_____	8.	_____
9.	_____	9.	_____
10.	_____	10.	_____
11.	_____	11.	_____
12.	_____	12.	_____
13.	_____	13.	_____
14.	_____	14.	_____
15.	_____	15.	_____
16.	_____	16.	_____
17.	_____	17.	_____
18.	_____	18.	_____
19.	_____	19.	_____
20.	_____	20.	_____

Rumplestiltskin
Key

1. Number of points on Queen's crown

2. Shape of points on Queen's crown

3. Position of sun

4. Flames on candles

5. Stripes on pillow

6. Number of small hearts on crib

7. Color of crib

8. Shape of crib rockers

9. Position of crown on baby's night gown

10. Position of feather in Rumplestiltskin's hat

11. Patch on Rumplestiltskin's right sleeve

12. Position of Rumplestiltskin's knife

13. Color of Rumplestiltskin's shirt

14. Stripes on Rumplestiltskin's tights

15. Color of Rumplestiltskin's shoes

16. Color of Queen's dress

17. Earring on Rumplestiltskin

18. Ring on Rumplestiltskin's left hand

19. Necklace on Rumplestiltskin

20. Knobs on crib posts

Sleeping Beauty

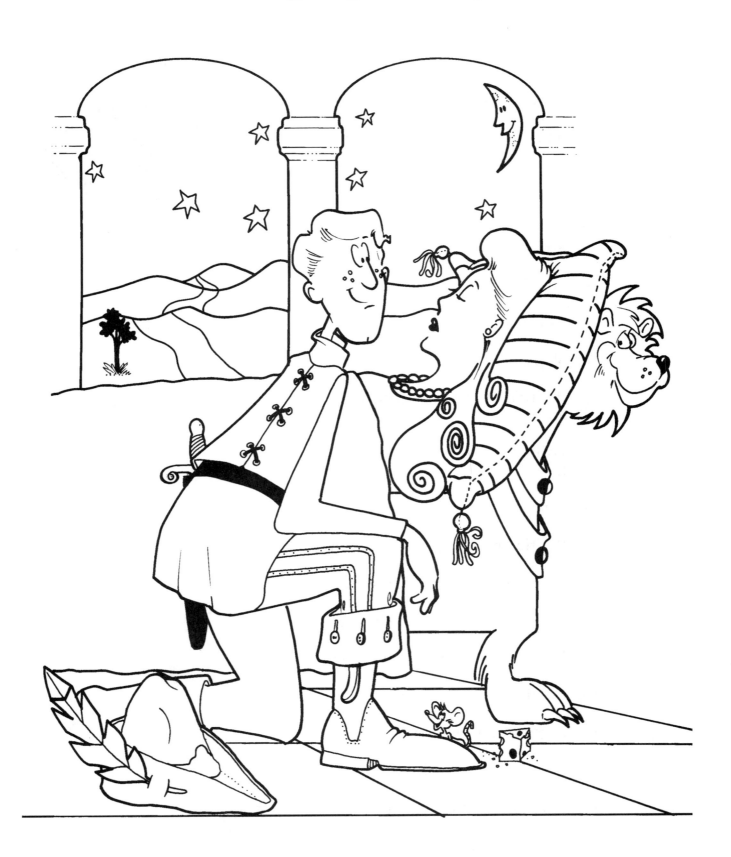

Sleeping Beauty

Sleeping Beauty

Answer Sheet

Same	Different
1. _____	1. _____
2. _____	2. _____
3. _____	3. _____
4. _____	4. _____
5. _____	5. _____
6. _____	6. _____
7. _____	7. _____
8. _____	8. _____
9. _____	9. _____
10. _____	10. _____
11. _____	11. _____
12. _____	12. _____
13. _____	13. _____
14. _____	14. _____
15. _____	15. _____
16. _____	16. _____
17. _____	17. _____
18. _____	18. _____
19. _____	19. _____
20. _____	20. _____

Sleeping Beauty
Key

1. Number of stars in sky

2. Number of trees on hills

3. Position of moon

4. Tassels on pillow

5. Sleeping Beauty's necklace

6. Stripes on pillow

7. Laces on back of Prince's vest

8. Stripe on Prince's pants

9. Buttons on ribbon hanging from bed

10. Color of Prince's boots

11. Number of buttons on Prince's boots

12. Position of cheese on floor

13. Position of mouse

14. Prince's sword

15. Color of tiles on the floor

16. Buckle on Prince's hat

17. Feather in Prince's hat

18. Freckles on Prince's face

19. Color of sky

20. Tassel on upper left of pillow

Snow White

Snow White

Snow White

Answer Sheet

<table>
<tr><th>Same</th><th>Different</th></tr>
<tr><td>

1. _____
2. _____
3. _____
4. _____
5. _____
6. _____
7. _____
8. _____
9. _____
10. _____
11. _____
12. _____
13. _____
14. _____
15. _____
16. _____
17. _____
18. _____
19. _____
20. _____

</td><td>

1. _____
2. _____
3. _____
4. _____
5. _____
6. _____
7. _____
8. _____
9. _____
10. _____
11. _____
12. _____
13. _____
14. _____
15. _____
16. _____
17. _____
18. _____
19. _____
20. _____

</td></tr>
</table>

Snow White
Key

1. Color of sky

2. Number of stars in sky

3. Position of candle

4. Flame on candle

5. Color of Snow White's hair

6. Position of pot in window

7. Number of wilted plants by window

8. Position of keys hanging

9. Number of keys

10. Buttons on Snow White's sleeve

11. Number of flowers on blanket

12. Patch on blanket

13. Color of stripes on sheets

14. Number & position of trees on hills

15. Safety pin/feather in right dwarf's hat

16. Position of rabbit

17. Feather in middle dwarf's hat

18. Snow White's bracelet

19. Bow in Snow White's hair

20. Number of knots in wood on head board

The Three Little Pigs

The Three Little Pigs

The Three Little Pigs

Answer Sheet

Same

1. _____
2. _____
3. _____
4. _____
5. _____
6. _____
7. _____
8. _____
9. _____
10. _____
11. _____
12. _____
13. _____
14. _____
15. _____
16. _____
17. _____
18. _____
19. _____
20. _____

Different

1. _____
2. _____
3. _____
4. _____
5. _____
6. _____
7. _____
8. _____
9. _____
10. _____
11. _____
12. _____
13. _____
14. _____
15. _____
16. _____
17. _____
18. _____
19. _____
20. _____

Same-Different: Fairy Tales® • Kagan Publishing • 1 (800) 933-2667

The Three Little Pigs
Key

1. Smoke coming out of chimney

2. Position of sun

3. Number of corn stalks

4. Window at top of house under roof

5. Color of highest pig's hat

6. Color of bricks on house

7. Position of basket

8. Knot in basket

9. Number of flowers on ground

10. Key hole

11. Size of ladder behind house

12. Color of Wolf's tale

13. Handkerchief in Wolf's back pocket

14. Color of Wolf's shoes

15. Wolf's tie

16. Color of lowest pig's hat

17. Flag on mail box

18. Panels on front door

19. Color of upper window

20. Color of lower window

The Tortoise and the Hare

The Tortoise and the Hare

The Tortoise and the Hare

Answer Sheet

Same

1. _____
2. _____
3. _____
4. _____
5. _____
6. _____
7. _____
8. _____
9. _____
10. _____
11. _____
12. _____
13. _____
14. _____
15. _____
16. _____
17. _____
18. _____
19. _____
20. _____

Different

1. _____
2. _____
3. _____
4. _____
5. _____
6. _____
7. _____
8. _____
9. _____
10. _____
11. _____
12. _____
13. _____
14. _____
15. _____
16. _____
17. _____
18. _____
19. _____
20. _____

The Tortoise and the Hare
Key

1. Number of apples in tree

2. Tongue in tree's mouth

3. Position of sun

4. Position of parrot

5. Color of Tortoise's sneakers

6. Spikes on Tortoise's sneakers

7. Bandaid on Tortoise's leg

8. Hare's pads on feet

9. Nail on starting blocks

10. Foot stops

11. Number of flowers on ground

12. Color of Tortoise's glasses

13. Number of circles on Tortoise's shell

14. Position and string on stop watch

15. Position of bottle & jump rope

16. Position of apple on ground

17. Tortoise's tail

18. Number of rocks on ground

19. Stripes on pole at start line

20. Number of trees on hills

Extra
Answer Sheet

Same

Different

Same	Different
1. _____	1. _____
2. _____	2. _____
3. _____	3. _____
4. _____	4. _____
5. _____	5. _____
6. _____	6. _____
7. _____	7. _____
8. _____	8. _____
9. _____	9. _____
10. _____	10. _____
11. _____	11. _____
12. _____	12. _____
13. _____	13. _____
14. _____	14. _____
15. _____	15. _____
16. _____	16. _____
17. _____	17. _____
18. _____	18. _____
19. _____	19. _____
20. _____	20. _____

Extra
Answer Sheet

Same

1. _____
2. _____
3. _____
4. _____
5. _____
6. _____
7. _____
8. _____
9. _____
10. _____
11. _____
12. _____
13. _____
14. _____
15. _____
16. _____
17. _____
18. _____
19. _____
20. _____

Different

1. _____
2. _____
3. _____
4. _____
5. _____
6. _____
7. _____
8. _____
9. _____
10. _____
11. _____
12. _____
13. _____
14. _____
15. _____
16. _____
17. _____
18. _____
19. _____
20. _____

Extra
Answer Sheet

Same

Different

	Same		Different
1.	_____	1.	_____
2.	_____	2.	_____
3.	_____	3.	_____
4.	_____	4.	_____
5.	_____	5.	_____
6.	_____	6.	_____
7.	_____	7.	_____
8.	_____	8.	_____
9.	_____	9.	_____
10.	_____	10.	_____
11.	_____	11.	_____
12.	_____	12.	_____
13.	_____	13.	_____
14.	_____	14.	_____
15.	_____	15.	_____
16.	_____	16.	_____
17.	_____	17.	_____
18.	_____	18.	_____
19.	_____	19.	_____
20.	_____	20.	_____

Extra
Answer Sheet

Same

Different

Same	Different
1. _____	1. _____
2. _____	2. _____
3. _____	3. _____
4. _____	4. _____
5. _____	5. _____
6. _____	6. _____
7. _____	7. _____
8. _____	8. _____
9. _____	9. _____
10. _____	10. _____
11. _____	11. _____
12. _____	12. _____
13. _____	13. _____
14. _____	14. _____
15. _____	15. _____
16. _____	16. _____
17. _____	17. _____
18. _____	18. _____
19. _____	19. _____
20. _____	20. _____

Notes

Notes